I0784066

The Tales, Tails, and Trails of Triple Creek

Andrea Todaro

RPSS - Rock Paper [Safety] Scissors Publishing
429 Englewood Avenue • Buffalo, New York 14223
www.rpsspublishing.com

ISBN: 978-1-956688-01-6   Hardcover
Printed in the United States of America

17 18 19 20 21   7 6 5 4 3 2

RPSS Publishing - Buffalo, New York

Dedication:

*This book is for all my "fine, feathered friends"
(you know who you are), my amazingly kind and
supportive mother and father, my entire family
and my loving boyfriend Brandon Wigley.*

*I hope you enjoy this silly, playful, meandering,
sometimes rhyming, and sometimes not
Dr. Seuss–like experience!*

Introduction

Built on 990 acres of conservation land in sunny Riverview, Florida,
the Triple Creek Community is teeming with wildlife of all varieties.
Triple Creek Preserve surrounds it, a combination of prairies,
woodlands, and swampy wetlands, joining the nearly 6,000-acre
Balm-Boyette Scrub Nature Preserve on its northern boundary. The
preserve holds more than 20 miles of bike and hiking trails
maintained by volunteers and is intersected by three tributaries to the
Alafia River — Bell Creek, Boggy Creek, and Fish Hawk Creek.
In this region of trails and tributaries is where I found myself during
that momentous year to remember. While coping during the
COVID-19 lockdown, I decided to write a book about the wildlife I
chanced upon during my nature walks.

Our environs take on a unique significance, life, and imagination all
their own when we serve as observers, interacting minimally with
them. This is especially true when taking the time to reflect on what
we've observed, seeing the creative potential and learning
opportunities in everything. When I first started writing, I thought,
what is there to be said about nature that hasn't been said before?"
Never a great fan of "lay-poetry," I wasn't sure if I could find
significance and intrigue in my poems. Yet, as I
rolled along, it felt like an effortless, rollicking
trip into a whole new world, an eco-system
that incorporates and even celebrates contrasts:
diversity and homogeneity, tradition and openness/change, ease and

survival/strain, ugliness and beauty. All these polarities co-exist for me in a seemingly comfortable, meaningful, and rich swirl of experience.

It was a refreshing departure from the excessive strain of political and public health divisiveness and technological complexity of our modern world. I found that I learned quite a bit from observing Florida wildlife through both an objective lens and that of the imagination. I was able to reach more deeply into myself, finding a vehicle for my desire for a better, happier, and more accepting world while embracing its built-in contradictions through poetic expression. You'll note that the poems often softly unfold into small doses of social commentary. This is my way of revealing inclinations and opinions on love and acceptance rather than advertise them. I try to show competing viewpoints, much as a visual artist shows contrast in light/darkness on the subject matter. In the quiet depths of my heart, I dream of a day when humans can cohabitate and mingle like rich, colorful, and diverse wildlife, accepting each other's differences. It's probably a "pipe dream," but I'd love it if we could all "have a cookie and be nice." (Winking at my friend Virginia McIntire here, who specializes in this.)

Yet, for those who are ultra "PC" or heavily analytical, don't try and look too deeply. My Cuban bullfrog poem is not an attempt to reveal my position on current US immigration policy. It's about frogs, damn it! I'm expressing that invasive wildlife can ruin a delicately balanced ecosystem if not kept in check.

On a side note, I was always a fan of Dr. Seuss and his unique vivacity coupled with a manipulation of everyday words and names to achieve rhymes. Therefore, I was pleased when perhaps noticing his writing style unexpectedly flowing into my work. Anyone who has known me for about five minutes will also notice the proliferation of puns popping into the conversation. Some are clever, while others admittedly prompt a "gag reflex" and a patronizing "that was a good one, sort of."

These puns, wordplays, and "Double Ent 'Andrea's'" make me happy… plain and simple. Through them, I long to make others feel similarly. Let's all learn not to take ourselves and others so seriously. It's much better to "crack people up" before they take flight to another perch, especially if they are looking a little sour-n-dour that day. It also helps us play better in the sandbox, dune, marsh, frog bog, etc.

This book is mostly for my family and friends - a loving, diverse, and harmonious breed who cannot easily be "pigeonholed." If there's one common thread between them, it's that I always leave their company feeling "well-fed" from good food and "food for thought." They are the greatest.

The Pelicans and Roseate Spoonbills

While venturing out beyond my usual stroll and taking a slightly more daring turn into the outskirts of our community near a local highway, I chanced upon the queerest sight. Scores of birds were lined up along a mangrove marsh as if poised for a yearbook photo – completely statuesque and awaiting my arrival. "The Pelican Junior League Photo Presentation" at first made me think that someone, as an odd joke, had stuck plastic figurines by the water's edge. (After all, this mangrove isn't too far away from a local trailer park studded with plastic pelicans and tacky lawn décor, giving the word "hick" true meaning.)

I waited and stood completely still before slowly approaching the ensemble, drawing in closer to capture the marsh's entire view. They remained like statues, tall and immutable. My eyes then rested on dozens of more pelicans perched on the marsh's inner banks, forming near-perfect tableaus as if they too had positioned themselves "just so."

But wait…a ho! There were two rosy-pink ones, rich with distinct markings yet not flamboyant or curvy enough to be flamingos. These large wading birds, whom I later identified as Roseate Spoonbills, are native only to the Western Hemisphere and recognized by their rosy color and unusual spoon-shaped, spatulate beak.

They were hunted to near-extinction in the late 1800s due to their uniquely colorful appearance. I was transfixed as the Spoonbills remained somewhat independent of the others, standing out as royal gems amidst the white pelican families. The pelicans held a strict allegiance to their group, conforming rigidly to their perch formations, while the more active Roseate Spoonbills freely moved around the group of white pawns like Queens on a chessboard.

Although my imagination initially created a hierarchy, upon closer observation, the pelicans seemed to live in perfect harmony with the Roseate Spoonbills, neither revering nor ostracizing them. Instead, they cohabitated seamlessly with this breed of unique temperament and color, remaining in stoic formations while allowing the Roseate Spoonbills, perhaps the artists of the bunch, to add splashes of color. Sometimes, the Spoonbills joined the group and froze in poses, while at others, they decided to dance and skim the water, creating small whirlpools that stirred up mud and all types of yummy insects and crustacean catches.

Although not all of nature is this amiable, amicable, and accepting, it felt exhilarating to co-exist for even a moment with birds of various feathers: those who prefer rules and conformity, others who like to color outside and blur the lines, some who appear plain-n-simple, and others who are vibrant by nature and have everyone be just fine. Quaker/Mormon pelicans and disco dancer spoonbills unite!

The Four-spotted Pennant Dragonfly

Swarming energetically as I approach you near Spanish moss and trees drinking from fresh-water ponds, I observe your "social distancing panache," soaring just a bit higher or off to the side as I come within 6 feet. After cyclists and runners have startled me and whizzed by without observing the same guidelines, I feel that the dragonflies have a lesson or two to teach about safety and politeness. Whereas they aren't territorial and don't "freak out" at the first sign of human intruders, they instead just graciously and gracefully skirt them, making minor shifts and recalibrations.

I can see why having a dragonfly land on one's head is considered good luck. It seems the likelihood of one doing so would be rare and therefore a special occurrence, given that they almost always appear in motion, veering deftly around humans in the Florida wilderness.

I was so pleased when a single dragonfly broke away from the swarm and zoomed over to perch on a tall reed, lingering long enough for me to get the perfect "glamor shot". It appeared to be delicately drinking in the sap, landing on it for several seconds before fleetingly fluttering away, diving and dipping, circling back, and then magnetized to the same reed again.

There is such variety of expression in these small circus performers with glistening wings. Swarms perform collective, synchronized dances, and happy soloists show their agility with dramatic swerves, shifts in motion, and arcs through the open air. Yet even these hyperactive, dizzying acrobats finally land in a balancing act occasionally. I wonder if this is what being in a continuous stream of ecstasy feels like? A wave of nostalgia hits as I remember one sultry summer in my early 20s… whirling and whizzing, sucking life's sweetness and rarely landing for long. Ah, but such is the life of a perpetually pleasing performer…a singing and soaring, dreaming and dancing dragonfly!

Sooty Tern

Never spurn a Sooty Tern
Just as I was amiss for something to write…
I spotted you around the next turn, Sooty Tern…
A big bold bird in a marshland sight
You made my heart yearn, Sooty Tern
Out of the blue, you put me back "in the pink"
Filled my poet pen with fresh, black ink…
To write with inspiration anew…
Until your next perch, you flew, Sooty Tern.
Dubbed by sailors with the name "Wide-Awake,"
Due to the harsh noises you often make,
Usually spotted in a nesting colony,
Your name "Ewa Ewa," in Hawaiian means "cacophony."
Your cries make the sea churn, twist and turn, Sooty Tern.
As I watch curiously from land, surrounded by whirling wind
and swirling sand.
My eyes and ears burn.
Your clashing, clamorous calls, create swells of storms and squalls
As the skies turn stern.
And I await your return, Sooty Tern.
You're a seabird inhabiting tropical ocean.
Losing yourself in a sea of emotion.
Grouping, swooping and diving in motion.
Breeding on islands in the equatorial zone.
Yet you now stand…statuesque, serene, silent and alone.
In the shimmering sand of the Florida marsh,
Near a shady grove in a climate less harsh…
Perhaps you could scrape up a tasty dinner
"Filet minnow" is bound to be a winner
Making friends with a toad or trout…
And discover what true country livin' is all about.
Then, when you're done savoring a meal with trout and toad
You can hang up a sign saying, "Welcome to my comfy, new pond…
my "swanky swamp tres beau," my beauty of a snooty, sooty abode."

Mesmerizing Monarch

Sweet, vibrant, teasing monarch.

Please carry me away with you on your wispy wings.

You appear to have infinite freedom to travel anywhere, changing direction at a moment's notice and attending to any inviting attraction striking your fancy.

You land on moist leaves and vines just long enough to be admired and have me drink you in, fluttering your wings like the consummate flirt of the animal kingdom, batting her eyelashes.

Your nomadic lifestyle and colorful, evolving nature make you the ultimate bohemian princess, traveling on the southern balmy blasts as much as 100 miles a day during your 3,000-mile migration.

You are all about the beauty of change and transformation, emerging and unfolding gracefully when coming into your kaleidoscopic potency. Your power lies not only in your rich, colorful tapestry but in the acceptance and embracing of impermanence that there is beauty in fragility and fragility in beauty.

You dance and play with me in the breeze, for just long enough to brighten my day, adding a splash of color like a new friend who meets me out in the warm sunshine and connects just long enough to make my heart flutter, before we both spread our wings and fly out into the world, generating cheer and goodwill. Yet, even though we have met only briefly, our hearts will be forever transformed and enlivened.

The Florida Frog and Cricket Chorus

Ladies and Gentlemen, we proudly present to you: "The Florida Frog-Bog Philharmonic and Cricket Chorus with Soloist Andrea Todaro"

Soon after dusk descends upon my Southern Florida community, I take a stroll on clear nights to each of the marshes and ponds, savoring the shimmering moon's reflection while listening to the swelling chorus of tropical frogs and crickets.

One night, knowing that only the owls and marsh life are listening, I decide to record their fascinating Fantasy in G Major and sing along, weaving in a simple counterpoint melody in the pitch-black night. The only applause comes from the trees swaying and shivering in the breeze, the flapping and clapping palm leaves, and shivering and quivering cypresses.

I've also likened those soulful calls and echoes to a tribal, meditation chant or techno/dubstep sample, as frogs harmoniously alternate simple rhythms and melodies. It might be fun to build them into a song, I think, but then feel that it would be quite silly! I wonder what they communicate to one another in the night's stillness under the moon.

Then, I grow concerned that I may only have these thoughts due to "quarantine boredom" and would not be so fascinated with marsh sounds if my life wasn't pared down to such simplicity.
Ah, but sweet simplicity it is, and it has me crooning and swooning! I never seem to tire of these beautiful orchestral sounds, alternating between harmony and unison, greeting me each night, curing any loneliness, and making me feel at peace, settled, and one with creation.

Blue Heron

Poised at a riverbank, the stately Blue Heron scans its watery domain for prey.

The breeze tickles and rustles its blue-gray feathers along with the long breeding neck and twin black head plumes.

I always find it amazing how these fierce, protective creatures alternate between long, deliberate steps with meticulous surveillance and striking like lightning to grab a fish or snap up a gopher.

Representing the tempest in nature and noble personality traits, they are powerful birds found in every part of the world. For example, they're considered "messengers" in Greek mythology, encouraging humans to evolve through self-determination.

They have a duality in Native American folklore, symbolizing good luck and patience and being portrayed as restless loners due to their solitary nature, except during breeding times.

As I stare at this self-reliant, magnificent Seminole Indian chief with his distinct, majestic markings, I wonder if it's possible to be a patient loner during pivotal times in one's life.

Does forced seclusion have to equate with weakness, apprehension, loneliness, and all the negative traits we ascribe to it?

If we can develop his far-seeing gaze, might we be able to envision a prosperous future while also feeling and visualizing our present interconnectedness?

Couldn't we, with patience and fortitude, channel the spirit of the Blue Heron surrounded by the sturdy Florida Everglades, making our way smoothly and gracefully to breeding season?

Yes, with his staunch, stern visage and regal posture, the Blue Heron teaches us something about preserving one's dignity through occasional inaction, moments of stillness, patience, and contemplation. Such times often lead to more significant growth and springing forth, as we gain an aerial scope of our surroundings and prospects from a higher perch.

Resting periods, which help us conserve energy, ultimately fuel our passion and desire. So, we patiently wait, and then when we see our target within reach, snag it and bag it.

Before the pandemic, I was in too much of a commotion of motion, swooping and flying back and forth, migrating between geographic and emotional states, and unable to create the patience, stillness, and space in my life to even write a simple poem, letting alone an entire score.

Yet, through forced circumstances, I'm able to sit and scan the water's depth for meaning, develop a more extraordinary gaze as I search the horizon, and learn to stand still in the wind, using this as a gestation period for fulfilling my desires – and ultimately, as an opportunity to act.

Florida Holly

The Florida holly or Christmas berry is blushing and reddening, its slight sheen beckoning me to admire and examine it in my fingers. Deriving its name from its fruit-laden branches and the small bright-red fruits maturing between December and January, it is often used in Christmas decorations in Florida.

As both my camera and eyes focus on it, I have these powerfully visceral flashbacks to a small, gold-gilded book I owned in my early 20s, which contained beautifully detailed paintings of fairies perched in trees and bushes at different seasons of the year. I used the fairy book as a reference for my creating my own sketches, and one of them, "The Holly Fairy," was of a delicate, androgynous fairy enchantingly straddling a holly branch with its arms crossed smugly. I remember how meditative it was, shading each berry a "pearly-red," making it shine and appear plump and juicy by giving it a spherical dimension. This cluster of holly also brought back memories of berry season and jam-making days in Buffalo, NY, my hometown.

Though pretty, shiny, and captivating appearing, later research revealed that this berry also has more austere qualities. It is part of the poison oak and ivy family, and sensitive people may develop severe dermatitis if their bare skin meets the sap or resins. Some people also report respiratory problems when the plant is in full bloom. In addition, it creates a dense forest canopy that shades out all other foliage, producing a poor habitat for native wildlife species by dominating over 700,000 acres in Florida.

Animals and humans still love the berry, despite its harshness. When dried, the berries are sweet, warm, fresh, and camphorous, the Pink Peppercorns in products such as McCormick Spice's "Peppercorn Mélange." Bees love the plant's flowers and make honey from their nectar. Raccoons, possums, and fruit-eating birds such as the Migratory Robin eat the plant's fruit and contribute to its spread. Some wildlife adores the berries for their narcotic effects.

Like the rest of life, the Florida Holly gives us the sour and the sweet, the sublime and the grime, the lemon, and the lime…it is a paradoxical mixed bag, making it compelling.

We are often attracted to the bright, shiny, and enticing surface… then peel a layer and reveal bare… a less comfortable experience. At this point, we can choose to be repelled, or we can linger longer and find more benefits, deeper meaning, and value. This is where life's nectar is revealed. So, let's make some pink peppercorns and sweet honey together, sugar.

Pink Muhly Grass

Pink Muhly Grass…sweet as a princess, or richly spun cotton candy…

As the breeze rustles your lavender-pink inflorescences, you greet me like rows of gently bowing and curtseying ballerinas, their soft, feathery tutus parting the path, which leads to perfection.

The music playing in the background is in perfect synch with your graceful swaying and bending dance, making me feel that nature choreographed it this way.

Your beauty explodes with sweetness, like puffy clouds of cotton candy. Although, I highly doubt you're edible, as my fingers fan your featheriness. You seem just for splash and show!

Maybe you are a long line of airy fairy-princesses, your feather dresses fanning and billowing, so as to have me drink you in and admire you. If so, am I to bow or curtsey?

I know! Let's celebrate each other… you acquiesce to me and my heart explodes in turn….beating with appreciation as your bursting color cheers and enriches my evening stroll, the sunset lying just be-yond, over the lake, as you slowly choose to reveal it.

Sunsets

"She was in love with the sunset. No one else ever even stood a chance."

A sunset in early spring in Florida is like a feisty kiss goodbye to daylight and a warm hello to night.

It's amazing how it flaunts so many different stages of bursting beauty…rapidly changing colors in a smooth slideshow; a quick, explosive love affair cools to sweet, mellow embers of twilight.

The pictures I took of it remind me of how my brain must light up while watching a sunset…or what it would look like if doctors were running a brain scan of a neurochemical rush.

But, let us reset to the magic of the sunset.

No longing is felt as the liquid sun slips and dips below the horizon. It's a smooth slideshow of perfection. We're merely observers of the skies' fiery orange and scarlet display…entranced in the peaceful afterglow, wherein lies bliss and wanting for nothing more.

Wandering trail of beauty

Although freshly manicured bike paths, walkways, and carved wooden bridges are pretty enough and overlook a vast expanse of bucolic beauty in our community, I prefer the remote paths tucked away at the outskirts.

For an extra daily dose of nature, I often cap off my ambitious five-mile walk with an enchanting trail slightly on civilization's edge. Every part of me feels more reverent and appreciative as I slip away into the trails tender fold of flora and fauna, unspoiled and untampered, save for its inhabitants.

Palmettos overshadow the trail, Spanish moss, berries and bushes of all budding varieties, gently winding through the wood, providing just enough safety to be close to society yet enough cover and natural beauty to be ensconced in one's primitive, private sanctuary. I smile at the sunlight streaming through and reflecting off the fanning leaves. My steps slow and soften as I feel soothed and connected with the larger woodland energy and its quiet depth.

A single thought breaks my submergence in the serene scene: "Oh, I hope no one else learns of this trail as I'd love to have it all to myself for a few magical moments in time." We know therein lies perfection, divorced from ideology or identity.

The path opens into a pleasing tapestry of grass, space, and sunlight. People are approaching quickly, getting ready to enjoy it. I don't mind. I've already had a lingering taste of breathtaking beauty and purification in woodsy solitude.

Where will you make a perfect space for yourself today in a world all your own, thoughts momentarily melting into sheer gratefulness, glee, and glory be? By accepting and being fed what nature longs to give us, our generosity from surplus flows.

The Wide-backed Broad-chested Andrea

She's found in lakes, marshes, parks, and fields

Intimidating all other creatures

For her size and stature demands them yield

As no animal could ever reach her

At first glance, she doesn't look so scary

Perhaps even a little inviting

That is, unless you're her adversary

Whom she'll easily strike down like lightning

There's much to be said about Andrea

Her looks, her style, her unique charm and grace

Often compared with the goddess Freya

Besides her giant frame and tiny face

Out in the wild she has no equal

And in my heart she soars like an eagle

- Brandon Wigley, guest poet

Neotropic Double-Crested Comorant

Arriving each day faithfully to sunbathe and fish at the community pond right outside our home.

You perch on a drainpipe mid-morning or evening when the sun's rays are "just right," not too dull or scorchingly bright.

The essence of majestic masculinity, you spread out your expansive, muscular wings, displaying your fierce black plumage and claiming your reign as "Purveyor of Pond Proceedings."

Absorbing the sun's rays, you command over the land from your drainpipe throne for long stretches.

The only distraction warranting a careful repositioning or short "leave of absence" from your throne is a trespasser coming too close or a yellow perch fish flapping, flipping, and flopping in the water. If a pedestrian gets too close, you move a bit out of range but not in a way that shows weakness or alarm. In fact, unless they set foot within a couple yards, you won't budge at all.

Yet, if you spy a yellow perch, walleye, or smallmouth bass fluttering under the water's surface, you are ready to move at a moment's notice. Then, you become an expert and calculated diver, swooping smoothly into the water, plunging and disappearing mysteriously into its depths…smooth as glass…black into black…

Cormorants are generally gregarious, nesting in colonies, gathering in flocks, and often also hunting together in groups, yet you are none of these things. Instead, you appear absorbed in your own regal worth, masculine ego, and self-care, flying, fishing, and perching solo style. It's as if the pond and surroundings are your sprawling bachelor pad…an estate with an endless food supply and opportunities to do nothing but preen, self-admire, and sunbathe.

Then, one morning, after weeks of seeing you on the same perch every day, you vanish, and we mourn the loss of your presence "ever so slightly," as we've gotten used to your faithfulness every day, your display as if you've been saying "Welcome to ME. I present to you ME in all MY perfection."

Later in the day, we spot you a block over, like a traitor, perched on a more considerable drainpipe in a luxurious, richer pond teeming with more excitement and wildlife. You've tricked us into thinking that you'll be faithful to our pond every day, yet your instinctual opportunism has prevailed.

We call you "HIM," not because of your occasionally wicked ways but because of your emboldened, confident masculinity. We revere your expert diving and fishing expeditions and commanding presence, which seems more like a true king presenting his kingdom rather than a bodybuilder vainly posing and flexing his muscles. So, we forgive you when you occasionally get bored, desiring a posher get-away.

We're grateful when you still grace us with your presence at our pond "most" of the time. And when you don't, we will meet and worship you where you are in the sun, basking and bedazzling by just "being."

Alligator Mash

She said, "See ya later alligator," well before the gator became a
traitor-n-ate'r.
Your menacingly toothy smile in cradle-shaped mouth, steers me
clear from ponds down South.
Seeing you swim in a lonely river, makes me tremble and twitch,
shudder and shiver.
Images burn into my impressionable mind…of the mysterious
predator left behind.
Yet, you are really a "docile crocodile," a "see-ya-later alligator".
Only when provoked, are you a heavy-breathing Darth Vader
An invader traitor who invad'er-n-ate'er.
No one other than a participating 'gater
Knows you can be quite a toothsome, woo-some and courting mater.
At the start of breeding season, young females, you'll be a'pleasin'
A rhapsody of water ripples from your rumbling bellows
Courtship catcalls, scores of roars and herculean "hellos,"
Snout-n-back rubbing; an alligator's version of men out "clubbing"
Bubble-blowing, body-showing…
Head-slapping, tail flapping.
Any device, naughty or nice…
To snag a mate that's "cream of the crop"
(But, please, make this stop! Get your gater out of the gutter…this
poem is starting to sputter)
A gater-grin saying "let me in;" a tongue flick? "My mind may be sick
but I'm quite the pick"
You grubby-gaters may "come on thick" and be full of "ick,"
But at least you don't send her a pic of your __ck!

Gardenia

Spilling forth and emoting your delicate, immaculate scent

Every part of your flowering bush is like a human's evolving state and levels of growth and consciousness, not happening all at once but in various stages.

Parts of you are still prickly – there's an old decaying bud closed off and containing the memory of what once was. Another pod is seemingly in early adolescence, not yet open and ripe to the world and still protected by soft, innocent fur.

Yet another seems middle-aged and full of toughness and solvency. Its soft and supple middle is surrounded by a rugged "been around the block" protective layer to keep others from getting close too quickly. It has not yet transitioned into an old, brittle and frail flower bud.

Lastly, of course, there's the ripe, unfolded, bursting, and rich flower, with the curves of womanhood, fully fragrant, vibrant, and alert.

Although the open, white flower is clearly the most alluring and expressive, all flower stages on the tree have equal importance to me - each contains a curious and rich story. There are different songs and stories, some enthusiastic, chattery, and verbose – some peaceful, resigned, and concise. Stages of life are fascinating, beautiful, and sacred…in people and flowering trees. And each year, each generation, the songs are reinvented and sung again…

Ode to Beauty in Southern Springtime

Sweet, flowering hibiscus…your petals rich and on display, splaying loosely and listlessly on a Southern Spring day.

Out in the bright, open sunshine, you absorb the divine… shimmering and rustling with excitement, you shiver in the early morning breeze, waking up to a fresh new start with a rich, open heart.

They call you a "weeping hibiscus" yet weeping is not your style…. Unless you receive a careless tear or two, from the fresh morning dew. You are too vibrant to feel sorrow…or be concerned for tomorrow… Laziness is more your "Southern charm"…as you roll and sway in the breeze, mesmerizing and captivating your audience effortlessly, reminding us of the infinite possibilities of beauty and art when we slow down, melt into our enchanting surroundings, and allow ourselves to be captivated by nature's majesty and magic.

Crisp, vibrant morning drifts into a muggy afternoon, your alertness lapsing into sluggishness as your branches' natural movements become more legato…sways stretching gracefully over longer periods of time…in harmony with the natural Floridian pace and way… Your soft, silken petals, which initially appear rich and bursting with readiness to greet the world, are really weeping and sleeping, drifting into simple dreams of perfect, sunny days with sandhill cranes napping beneath your branches and puffy clouds drifting without at-tachment or meaning…just basking in the "beingness" and "belong-ness"…like a young child in the rich expanse of the world, merely one with it and the easy rhythms of the day.

Sandhill Cranes

Cranes of a Feather Flock Together…those Gentle Sandhill Cranes

On a windy, golden evening….

Your elegance and slow, deliberate stride are unmatched…you have a regality about you - an "I own the place even if you live here," yet you are casual and relaxed monarchs of our community unless provoked to action.

You're always spotted in amicable pairs and seldom seen solo. I've most recently spied you strolling like a pair of lazy, lackadaisical lovers, before becoming momentarily eclipsed by the drooping Spanish Moss only to emerge by a busy, buzzing and swaying wonderland of wildlife marsh.

Feeling a little like a voyeur, I "crane" my neck, you captivate me so. I watch you drift closer to the water as you peer out over a lake fringed with cattails and Florida Gulf-Coast wildflowers, absorbing the view before making your evening ascent up a meandering walking trail. Surefooted and confident, your bodies appear to fleetingly form the shape of a heart as you lean into each other. Are you gazing lovingly and knowingly, or was it just my overactive imagination wanting you to be more human?

I marvel at your coordination, as you traipse down the long, winding cement path leading to a narrow wooden bridge, overlooking the entire pond and sky. Just as I hope that you will stop to take in the same expansive and overwhelmingly gorgeous view I experienced minutes earlier, you both communicate through a loud, instinctive cry, and quickly soar off into the open sky, making me realize our distinction and wish I could fly. It is at this moment, when we realize that as humans, no matter how free or confident we think we are, we are still bound by the limiting laws of nature.

During a balmy, blue-skied afternoon…

Now, there are not just one pair but several leisurely cranes studding the long islands and walkways of our Triple Creek Community, curled up and resting under trees, preening feathers, and digging with long beaks for a juicy prize. I walk confidently over to them, maintaining a respectful distance yet being tempted to draw closer and challenge the boundaries, as I'm often won't to do. I absorb the gulf breeze, which buffers the effects of the beating sun, feeling radiant and invincible while listening to some "feel good" meditation music, which momentarily makes my dopamine and endorphins explode.

The sandhill cranes, however, are anything but radiant or enthused about the day as they seek shelter under the sweet palmettos and Spanish moss, alternating between listless and obsessive. Some appear not easily roused and seem to have trouble opening even one eye as humans pass by, while others nervously dig and preen, almost appearing neurotic in their search for buried treasure. As the heat from the afternoon seems to make them more self-contained and absorbed, I'm reminded once again, that no matter how confident or free we appear, we are still bound by the limiting laws of nature…

Even my happy-go-lucky cranes! I'm also reassured of all life's rhythms…that there's a time to be free, a time to hunt, a time to preen, a time to fly and definitely a time to be lazy. Today, I choose the last one by observing cranes and writing poetry!

Turtle Truisms

Creepy, creviced turtle gets a "mug shot" near the crape myrtle.
"Charged with unattractive glares and outrunning hares.
Convicted of murdering mollusks and minnows."

You're technically a "terrapin," living out of ponds and within.

If scooped up by a clever captor near a crosswalk or mushy marshland,

You'd be swallowed entirely, fitting into any gentle lumberjack's hand.

Your face isn't prettily painted, no you ain't no turtledove

Puffed up on soft, cumulus clouds, with stary eyes of love.

Billing and cooing, courting and wooing…

Despite your lack of outer allure, your strong soul will endear and

endure…

Dating back to the dinosaur, you live and thrive forevermore.

Woah, as far back as 20 million years ago, you go!

You are masters at survival and self-selection.

Your hard-shell shields with self-protection.

Symbol of a long, well-lived life on mother earth,

A balanced pace and gentle birth.

One of the oldest reptiles, strength unfurled,

Swimming in a sea underworld.

Predating snakes, crocs (yes, the animal and the shoes), insti"gators,"

and other traitors.

A reminder that you need to have trust in your way of working

things out.

Others may hasten, scream and shout!

But you needn't be tempted

To rush in movements with attacks pre-empted.

Instead, you carefully observe all details, then patiently proceed.

For a thoughtful, enduring soul is a wise, trusted turtle indeed.

The Cuban Tree Frog

Invasive and pervasive

With mating calls, persuasive

Mysterious and recondite.

Emerging on a moonlit night.

By day, you easily become part of a tree…

Drifting into serene anonymity.

Yet once dusk slowly, softly descends,

The racket you kick up never ends.

You sound more like a squeaky door or squooshy shoe than a frog.

When I've lingered at a boozy, buzzing bog on my midnight jog.

Nightlife in its heyday wouldn't be complete…

Without a firefly strobe light, and techno bug beat.

Yet, not one of you interacts with other frog-frats.

You're far more elite.

You're a load of a toad of spoiled brats.

That would do well to return to Cuba, in spats with your other ex-pats.

You feel a strong sense of entitlement.

And pose a threat to our environment.

It's interesting that I don't feel that way about people…

But I do feel so about the invasive frog and toad…

Who cling to my windows, hot tub, and inside my abode.

In fact, I even found one near my porcelain Goddess commode.

And another, looking all comfy inside my fresh laundry load.

I was going to put on my pants like I always do, one leg at a time.

When, suddenly, out popped this Cuban Tree Frog, less than sublime.

But before he decided to vanish.

Gesturing and speaking in rapid Spanish

He asked me where he could get the best Cuban sandwich.

While intermittently puffing on his Cuban cigar,

I gave him directions to Doug's Dive and Suzy's Sand Bar.

Where you could find a mini-Mosquito-Mojito with nice twist of lime.

And the best nightlife, salsa swamp music, and wild thyme.

So Cuban Tree Frogs are social and like to "wiggle their behind"…

With humans, bar "flies," and their own fetching froggy kind.

Loving Lily Pads

Lily Pads: the lily and the lotus are prettier and more powerful than the police and the POTUS.

I love how the lily pads float like loose, delicate lace draped on the water's surface. Spring's warmth beckons the leaves of water lilies to the calm surfaces of ponds, lakes, and slow-moving streams. They make an enchanting wonderland of marsh even more like an impressionist painting, ponds brushed and dusted over with soft, shiny ornaments.

Although they look merely decorative, lily pads serve a valuable purpose in the pond's eco-system. There is a lot going on beneath their placid surface.

They provide safe and clever hiding places for frogs from underwater predators. They also produce natural oxygen, which allows fish to breathe and beneficial bacteria to thrive, shading and keeping the water cool for its mysterious pond life.

As the natural "pond-patrol," solid protectors and defenders, they cover in a calm blanket of love and nourishment, forming a gentle bond of equanimity - a survival feedback loop of reciprocity where everyone wins!

Wouldn't it be amazing if we could feel this way about each other and such riches could trickle down more from the top?

A Pack of Quacks

On a shiftless summer afternoon, Florida's sweet and diverse
waterfowl appear unfazed by the heat and immersed in the feat of
flipping and dipping…waddling and wading, floating and feeding…
Strutting on land and gliding smoothly as elegant skaters on the
water's surface, they create mirror reflections and then mar them,
drawing circles and ripples with their movement.
So far, I've seen mallard, mottled, black-bellied whistling, white-
crested, and wood ducks cohabitating in cheerful harmony, relatively
unfettered by my presence and making enough space for us all.
They seem to celebrate the innocence and natural diversity – black,
white, black and white, green and white, brown with blue fringe, each
immersed in an array of land and lake "give-n-take."
I watch a single solid-colored duck dock next to several patch-quilt
ones – each seeming content with their own adventures.
Resting and swimming spots provide a bevy of rich secrets and
untapped fortune beneath the surface.
Aquatic and land insects, snails, worms, slugs, and other fun prey
keep the ducks perched and pre-occupied all day.
Though I notice that they sometimes fiddle-n-faddle, they usually
don't dawdle while they waddle off to piddle-n-paddle.
Once afloat, with a thump of the rump and upside-down dunk of the
throat and the coat,

Each dabbling duck tests his luck in the pond's coolness and muck
With a dip-n-dive, an unabashed "bottoms-up," skimming for food
in overdrive
In a desperate mood, all those mooning derrieres could be construed
and viewed as a tad bit rude.
It always makes me smile for a while.
When I see a duck so self-immersed that he doesn't care if his
bottom goes up last or pops up first.
Or even at all…either way, it just looks like they're having a ball.
I have noticed she seems particularly inclined…to pay no mind when
exposing her feathered behind…
Although I'm sure they just patiently wait to spot a floundering fish
in a sad-n-sorry state.
I still wonder what makes a particular "quack" stick out his bottom
ahead of the pack…
And be a "let's get a wee bit wetter" go-getter trendsetter.
Being the first plucky, ducky dude to plumb the pond for fresh fish,
ferns, and fancy fowl food.

About the Author: Andrea Todaro

Andrea Todaro, a Western New York native, is an artist, opera singer, and the president of Innovative Placements, a company that helps individuals with disabilities find employment. While isolated at her winter retreat in Riverview, Florida, during the COVID-19 outbreak, she decided to make the very best of her circumstances by regularly walking the nature trails and researching the conservation land wildlife of her Triple Creek Community. As an only child, she very much enjoyed the company of her stuffed animals and watched them come alive in her imagination.

While in Florida, the wildlife took on a similar whimsical, magical and comforting role. In fact, even some of the pesky, invasive species like the Cuban Bullfrogs became her new friends and shared a Cuban sandwich with her. She felt wholly embraced by her wonderful new family on the conservation lands without her human family and friends.

With over twenty years of professional job placement experience, Ms. Todaro has demonstrated a unique talent for matching over 3000 clients to the hiring requirements of many area employers.

In addition, she has served on the Buffalo Niagara Human Resource Association (BNHRA) board of directors in various roles, including Workforce Readiness, Diversity and Inclusion, and Membership

Director. She is also a member of The Society for Human Resources Management (SHRM) and has a Master's Certificate in Human Resources from Villanova University.

She has also served on committees and boards dedicated to supporting operatic talent in the WNY community, including the Opera Foundation of Buffalo and the local Met Opera Audition committee. Finally, she has planned and coordinated many health-n-wellness workshops, job fairs, and workforce readiness events. Helping others in any capacity is very "near-n-dear" to her heart, and she hopes to leave this world years later with a smile on her face due to this mission.

In her spare time, Ms. Todaro enjoys singing in concerts and operas. In addition to performing in many local theatre productions for 25 years, she has traveled twice to Italy to sing lead roles in the operas "Gianni Schicchi" and "Don Giovanni." She has also performed roles in operas and concerts in New York City and Central Florida.

As mentioned earlier, she dedicates this book to all her "fine, feathered friends" – (you know who you are), her amazingly kind and supportive mom and dad (Sarah and George Todaro), and her loving boyfriend, Brandon Wigley. You'll see that he makes a special appearance as a "guest poet" in this silly, playful, meandering, sometimes rhyming, sometimes not, Dr. Seus-like book!